WHEN YOU CAN'T LET GO 2

DAMAGED LOVE SERIES BOOK 2

MIA BLACK

CHAPTER 1

Jericka

"Hello?" came the deep voice from the other end of the phone. I was laying in my bed, headphones in my ear. I knew that it was stupid but I should have just opened my mouth to say something, anything at all. I felt like I was my teenage self all over again or something.

I had to admit that I was a little turned on by the voice. It was so sexy and sure of itself. I got a flash of Marco in my mind. His long dreads and beautiful complexion paired with that nice personality did something to me that I couldn't explain. It was sexual for sure but there was something else there.

It was such a strange set of circumstances that led to me laying there, calling another man and debating whether or not I was going to actually say anything to him or if I'd just end up hanging up and being a punk.

I'd been with my man Hov for more as long as I could remember. We'd been together since we were teenagers. He was the love of my life, or he used to be. I had trouble at times figuring out how I felt about him these days. Everything with us was good until he started using and abusing hard drugs and became abusive. He had gone and gotten himself locked up for being high and crashing into another car. I couldn't believe that he'd done it. It really was just a sign of how far down he had fallen. The worst part was that him falling from grace meant that he was dragging me and our son down with him. I didn't know what the future held for us, but my son was my first priority and I wasn't about to let Hov take Jasheem and I down with him.

Hov had gone out and done some real

stupid shit that had now put all of us into jeopardy and once again I had to be the one to pick up the pieces. I was at the strip club, working like normal, but hoping that it would be a good night. Hov had made it clear to me that he wanted me to be at his bail hearing and that hopefully I'd have the money he would need to get bailed out. We didn't have any real goals about how much I should make but I wanted to try and make as much as possible so I could get him out.

While at the club I was on stage doing my thing when I somehow crossed paths with Marco. Marco had to be one of the sexiest guys I'd seen in a while. He was tall with these long, beautiful dreadlocks. He was all muscular and shit. He was handsome as hell and when we went into the back, I danced for him and we ended up talking. Something about the way he moved turned me on. He was a mystery to me but something in me told me that he was a boss. He made it clear that he was interested in me and gave me his number, telling me to call him when I was ready for my life to change.

I'd had the number for a little while. I didn't

even plan on calling. It crossed my mind that I should call because I was home bored. Jasheem and I had spent the whole day at my best friend's house cause I wasn't trying to be in an empty ass house all day long. When I got home I called Marco.

"Yo?" The deep voice on the other end of the phone snapped me from my thoughts. I sat there with my headphones in my ear thinking I should say something when another thought crossed my mind. For years I'd been loyal to Hov. When he was good and on top, I was there. Now shit with us had switched gears and I was the one doing the work and bringing in the money. Was I not as tough as I thought I was? Yeah, Hov was in a fucked up position and stuff but it wasn't nothing too crazy. He hadn't even been officially charged and there I was...trying to chat with the next dude. I felt guilty as hell.

"I'm sorry. I got the wrong number," I said. I quickly hung up the phone and put it down. I stared at it for a couple of seconds, seeing if he'd call back, but he didn't. I couldn't believe I hadn't been smart enough to just block out my number. Marco would probably figure out that it was me one way or another.

I knew that stuff with Hov and I had taken a turn for the worst but I wasn't at that level yet. I wasn't about to try and talk to someone else, even if they realized the bullshit I was going through and was trying to help me out of it. I just needed to focus and spend my time working and taking care of Jasheem. I prayed that everything with Hov worked out but in the meantime I needed to focus on me and Jasheem. I laid in my bed, catching up on something on Netflix while drifting off to sleep.

The next day I spent with Jasheem. He'd asked about Hov and I really hated lying to him but it was what was best for him in that situation. I didn't want to have to explain to Jasheem that Hov was locked up in jail currently and could be for even longer if his bail got denied or something. Jasheem was smart but he was still a baby. He was only five years old. It was up to me to decide what was best for him until he got to an age where he could do it himself.

I was in my bedroom that evening, throwing stuff into my bag in an attempt get ready for work. I didn't want to be there too early but I hoped that getting there early would let me make some extra money.

"Mommy, I'm ready," said Jasheem. I turned around and he had his bag in his hand. My handsome little man with his dark brown skin and bright eyes was all ready to go to my mother's house.

"Good job big boy," I said. "You got all your toys for the night?"

"Yeah," he said.

"OK," I said. "Mommy is gonna finish getting ready. Go watch cartoons until I come out and get you."

Without another word he turned and headed down the hall to the living room. I heard him turn the TV on and one of those shows that he really liked came on.

I finished getting ready, throwing one more outfit into the bag. I grabbed Jasheem and we headed to my mother's house. Once we got there, I headed inside.

"You ready for work?" My mother asked. She poured out a cup of coffee. I wasn't normally a coffee drinker at all. My mother drank it all the time but it did help me a little when I did drink it.

"Ma, it's too late for you to be drinking

coffee," I said. "It's almost 8 o'clock. You know it's gonna keep you up."

"It ain't for me," she said. "You think I don't see them bags under your eyes? You gotta wake up." She may not have been too crazy about what I was doing but my mother also understood that at the end of the day you had to do what you had to do to support your family. It was that same hustlers' spirit that I'd gotten from her.

"Thanks ma," I said. I hadn't planned on staying too long but I decided to drink the coffee. I took a seat.

"No problem," she said. "I'm still here whenever you wanna talk about whatever is going on with you."

"I know ma," I said as I sipped on my coffee. It was black with just a little bit of milk and three sugars, just the way I liked it whenever I did have one.

My mother and I sat around for a couple more minutes while we talked about nothing in general. It was cool for us to just talk. I still wasn't ready to talk to her about the stuff that I had going on with Hov but it was always great to just sit and talk with her. After a while I kissed her on the cheek and headed to work.

While driving to work, I had a couple of minutes alone that I used to think about stuff. I was so damn confused in thinking about things. *Sorry to call, wrong number*, repeated itself in my head. That was so stupid. I'm sure that Marco knew it was me. I almost wondered if I'd end up seeing him tonight at the club but who knew. I wasn't thinking too much about him though. I had other thoughts. It had kind of annoyed me that I had the time to try and call Marco but I hadn't really been speaking to Hov like I should have.

Hov had been calling me from the jail and I hadn't been answering. I honestly had no real reason why not. I knew that Hov was probably calling to make sure that I'd been working and stuff but for whatever reason I just hadn't answered. I had a lot of stuff on my plate, between him, Marco, stuff at home, and everything else. I planned on going to the bail hearing and stuff to make sure that I was supporting him. I knew he would probably want me to come and bring Jasheem but I wasn't planning on bringing our son to some courthouse to sit around all day.

I got to the club and walked inside, greeting the security guards as I came in. They did their typical stuff, being respectful but also letting me know I looked good. I hadn't even dressed for work yet. I had on a pair of jeans and a t-shirt. I knew a lot of these bitches came dressed and ready to hit the stage but I wasn't trying to do all that. I carried myself differently than a lot of them.

I had gotten all the way dressed, wearing a red outfit and matching shoes. I was in the mirror, making sure I wasn't ashy when one of the girls walked up. Her name was Alexis. She was a pretty brown skinned girl with a small gap in her teeth. It wasn't too big though so it worked for her.

"How's it looking out there?" I asked her. She came in with a handful of money. She put it down in front of the vanity and sat down next to me. That was how she and I became cool. She ended up coming and taking the seat next to me when she first started and we became cool from there. We'd leave work and go out to breakfast some times before we went back home.

"Girl, it's crowded," she said. "I don't know who's in town or what but it's a lot going on tonight. Mad heads out there."

"Oh word?" I got a little excited. I couldn't help it. I was the same as anyone else in that regard; I wanted money.

"Hell yeah," she said. "I was barely able to make it to the stage. I did three dances before I got on. I had to send one of the new chicks to the stage to cover for me while I finished up."

"Damn, it's busy like that?" I said. I was definitely feeling a lot better about being there. When you strip you made your money on tips and half the dudes that came wanted you to bug out on the pole for them to only throw a dollar or something like that. I wasn't with it. I was always happy when we had new customers in the club cause they usually came ready to spend money.

"Hell yeah," she said. "It's early but we only got two tables left. Everything else is either reserved or already in use."

I nodded my head in approval. "Sounds good," I said. I climbed out of my chair and checked myself out in the mirror again. "I'm about to head out there. See you in a few girl."

"Make that money boo," she said with a smile.

Alexis hadn't been lying at all. I walked out into the glitz and glam that was the main floor of the club, past the curtains that separated the back area from the main parts and I was surprised by how packed it was. It had been weeks since I'd seen the place this packed. There must have been a concert...or a major drug deal happening that weekend. With Chicago you just never really knew which one it was.

It was packed with people. The bar was like a madhouse with people all reaching over one another trying to get their drinks. It looked like everybody was gonna eat tonight cause it looked like people had come ready to spend money.

I'd barely been out on the floor for a minute before a dude approached me for a dance. I did it. I wanted to just test the waters and see what he was trying to spend. It wasn't much but it was a nice little $40 to start off the night. It definitely put me in the mood to do more.

I managed to get in a couple more dances before it was my time to hit the stage. Being on the stage could be annoying as hell at times but it was my honestly my favorite place to be. I was never the attention seeking type when I was growing up but I liked being on the stage cause of all the attention it provided me with. Stripping was selling a fantasy. The best and easiest way to sell it was for me to have the attention of the whole damn place. I made sure that when I was up there that I put on a show. I always switched back and forth between fast and slow songs because I wanted to keep it as fresh as I possibly could. The owner of the club had even sent a couple of the new girls my way a few times so that I could show them the ropes if they'd never done it before.

The DJ announced me and the music started to play. I switched it up and danced to some reggae. This artist that I liked had just come out with a new song so I gave it to the DJ to play for me. I wanted to make sure that I was the first chick in the club to dance to it before it became bigger. I moved my hips like I was trying to hypnotize the crowd. I shook my body and let the lights hit my skin as it shined under them. No shade but I went off on that stage. I was doing all types of shit. I was moving, shaking, making it clap, and more. All the thoughts that I had in my head came out as I danced. I used my emotions to make me move better. It was the only place that I could really think of that let me be as carefree as I wanted. I climbed the pole and let it drop into a split.

I stood back up and turned around to face the people. I looked at them all, spotting a couple of people I knew. I looked through the crowd and felt a little twinge of something in my stomach when I saw him. Marco was standing there, well sitting there at the bar. He had a couple of people with him this time around. Two of them were talking to him and he was listening because he nodded but his eyes were on me. It was the same way it was the other night, him staring at me like he was in a trance. I kept on dancing, trying to ignore him and what not but every now and then my eyes would drift off to him and he was still staring.

Just like last time, Marco tipped well. The club was packed which meant that I had more money than the other night but Marco had been throwing money at me like crazy too. I didn't know what he did for a living but he was throwing that cash like he was printing it himself. I grabbed my money, took it to the back and hid it, and then came back out to the floor, searching for my next dance.

I hadn't meant to run into him but I'd somehow literally walked right into Marco. He looked just as good as the other night, keeping it simple in a pair of jeans and a white t-shirt. He had on a gold rope chain that hung loosely over his thick, muscular neck. His dreads were wrapped up in a bun behind his head. There was something sexy about the way he moved. I didn't know what was going on with us but I didn't know how I felt about it.

I had to admit that I had mixed feelings about seeing him again. Yeah I was attracted to him and all but my mind just wondered about him a lot. I didn't know what he was doing there. Had he come to see me? Was he going to try and get me to dance for him again? What was he after? If Marco and I ended up getting cooler I'd definitely make sure to ask questions about him. He didn't seem like a big talker but I could get him to say something.

"Wassup Jericka?" he greeted me, looking a little happy to see me. He smiled just a little bit, just enough to make it clear that he was being friendly only for me though. His friend opened his mouth to say something to him but Marco just held up his hand and stopped him. Yeah, he was a boss. I needed to know more about him.

"Hey," I said. I wasn't trying to sound too friendly. I wanted to know that this time around it was just about the business. I didn't know if I believed that part myself, not with all that had happened with us before.

"You did ya thing on the stage," he said. His deep voice sounded loud over the music of the club. "You got moves for real."

"Thank you," I said.

"You tryin' to head to the back with me?" Marco asked.

I had to admit, I was a little nervous about heading to the back with him for a lap dance. I knew that last time we were back there we made a connection and stuff. Plus, it was obvious that he and I had some sexual tension between us. I wasn't trying to get back there and have something happen between us. The shit that ultimately made me decide to go to the back with him was the fact that he was a good tipper and I needed the money for Hov.

"Ok," I said to him.

We headed to the back where the private rooms were. I spotted a couple of other girls who'd just left from back there. One or two of 'em nodded or smiled at me, probably knowing that Marco was about to throw some money my way. They looked happy themselves. There must have been something in the air that night that made everybody wanna come and spend all their money at the club. It wasn't the first or the fifteenth.

Marco paid the fee for the dance and we headed into the small room. I went ahead and started dancing for him. My mind was else-where though. I'd only been dancing for a couple of minutes but I could tell that Marco knew something was up. Whenever I turned around and looked at him, his eyes were focused on my face and not my body. I knew that it had to be coming across as bad but I had mad other shit on my mind.

"Hold up," Marco said. He held up his hands. I stopped dancing and turned to look at him.

"What's wrong? You good?" I asked him. I

still hadn't gotten all the way naked. I had on my panties still.

"Yeah. I'm good but are *you* good?" he asked me. He was looking at me with confusion all over his face.

"What you mean?" I asked him. I knew that I'd been distracted but I didn't think that it was enough to have him notice it.

"It's something wrong with you," he said. "I told you that you could call me if you need to talk or something. I hope it ain't your dude fuckin' up again or something."

"It's cool if I sit?" I asked him. He nodded at me and he moved just a little bit so I could be comfortable.

I took a seat at the edge of the chair next to him. I took a deep breath. "I did call," I said to him.

His eyes got all narrow and then he looked at me and just nodded his head. "Oh, that was you with the wrong number shit, huh? I thought so. I thought I recognized your voice. Why you ain't say something?" Marco asked me and he laughed a little bit too.

"Marco look, I don't want you to get the wrong

impression about me. Yeah I strip and all that but I'm not one of these money hungry bitches that works in here. I think you're cool. You're handsome and all that. You're easy to talk to. The thing is, I ain't never been nothing if not loyal. Hov may not be too much but I'd be a disloyal ass bitch if I left him when he needed me the most," I said.

Marco just nodded his head. "Just chill out," he said and he smiled at me. "Look, I get that. I ain't trying to do nothing you don't wanna do. I like you and you cool as shit but I wouldn't try and take you from your man. I wouldn't get with you if I could do that cause all it would take is the next nigga to take you from me. You loyal. I just seen too many people in situations like yours. Your dude is gonna fuck up and when that happens, hit my line. You feel me?"

I nodded my head. "Yeah," I said with a slight smirk. I couldn't figure this dude out. I made a mental note to ask Tamika about him. She did hair so she always got all the gossip from people. I'd never seen Marco before that other night at the club but he seemed like someone people just knew. When I was on stage a couple of people tried to talk to him but he waved them away and just focused on me.

"Cool," he said. He reached into his pocket and pulled out another one hundred dollar bill. "That's for you."

I took the money from him and thanked him. Marco got up and reminded me that I should hit him up if I needed anything. I told him I would.

CHAPTER 2

Hov

The worst part about being locked up besides the fact that you weren't free was the fact that it was very easy to get bored. This wasn't prison or anything big like that. It was only the county lock up which meant that all we had to do all day was look at one another. Yeah, we had a couple of card games and shit to play but that was mostly it. I'd played more games of spades in there in the last two days than I had in the last two years.

My mind was starting to feel like it was going numb or some shit. I hoped that shit went good on Monday so that I could get out. It was only two days away but it felt like two months. I hoped Jericka had been out there hustling for me like she said she would be.

Jericka and I had a bond that a lot of other people didn't really understand. Niggas nowadays got with a shorty like that and everything was good while they were on top. Jericka was the quality type of woman. If she didn't live in Chicago, I could see her being the wifey type to an NBA baller or something like that. She had a really good heart and cared about people in a real way.

When we first got together I was still a little boy who thought he was a man. I loved her cause we got a chance to grow together. Everything we had and the shit that we still have, we built it together. I didn't have to worry about shit cause I knew that she'd hold me down. It was what she always did.

At least with me being in there and knowing more than a handful of people I hadn't had any trouble. Like I said, it was only county lock up. Niggas in there were waiting for trials and stuff like that. They weren't trying to fuck up what could be their last little taste of freedom by getting into a fight over some dumb shit. For the most part I just stayed inside my cell though. I wasn't trying to make new friends in there. The thing about jail was that everybody came in with a different set of circumstances. Some people came in cool and just wanted to do their time with their heads down. Other times niggas came in there and just wanted to wild out cause they were so used to being on the inside.

"It started yet, young blood?" Speedy's voice made my eyes snap open. We were both in our cell. It was after the evening count and lights out. I'd been laying there for the last hour trying to go to sleep but it just wasn't coming to me. I don't know where I'd gotten that shit from but something was making me feel sick as hell. I was sweating and all that like I had a fever.

"Shut the fuck up," I snapped at him. Speedy was cool for an older dude but I didn't need that nigga checking on me.

Speedy had told me all about his drug problem and shit. He told me that I was gonna turn into him if I didn't get my shit together. I wanted to tell him about I wasn't as bad as him though. He kept acting all old and wise like he was some old kind of drug guru or something like that. He was cool but he was starting to get on my nerves with that shit.

The other thing he'd said was starting to come true though. He told me that I was gonna end up going through withdrawal symptoms. I hated to admit that I was that far gone but I figured out that was what was happening to me then. I'd just been feeling out of it since I woke up that morning. It was like I'd somehow gotten a bad cold but I knew that it had to be the damn drugs leaving my system and my body calling for more.

"Yeah whatever," Speedy said.

"It's a cold," I said to him. I sniffled and turned to my side.

"Sure," said Speedy. I heard the bed squeak which must have meant that he was turning over. I was glad too. I needed that nigga to mind his business.

After another hour or so I finally managed to drift off to sleep. I didn't know how long I slept for but I woke up feeling bad as shit. I felt like somebody threw my body into a blender or some shit. I was all kinds of fucked up. I was achy, sweaty, and just everything bad.

I needed to go see the nurse, the doctor,

somebody. Something was wrong with me. I'd been to rehab a couple of times but they always made sure that I had some medicine that made the withdrawal symptoms a lot better. I'd never have just gone through it cold turkey the way that I was doing then. I slowly climbed out of the bed, my whole body aching when I did it. I felt horrible.

I walked to the bars of the cell, glad that a guard happened to be walking by. He was one of them big ass football player looking type of dudes. He was taller than me and wider too.

"Yo," I called out to him. I leaned on the bars, holding on to them to help me stand up. I didn't know what the fuck was going on. My heart was pounding in my chest. I was sure that someone else could hear it. It was moving mad fast and beating hard too.

"What?" he stopped and turned to look at me. He had this blank expression on his face. I guess they weren't allowed to show emotions and shit like that. I didn't care though. I didn't need that nigga to be my friend or even to like me. He just had to take me to the hospital.

"I need to see the doctor," I said. "My heart…it's beating too fast." I said. My stomach felt like the fucking Olympics was going on with all those backflips and shit happening.

"Not this shit again," he said. "Let me guess, your body hurts too?" The guard smirked like he was glad I was in pain.

I just nodded my head. It felt like it was getting harder to stand up. "Yeah man. You gonna take me or what?" I asked. I wasn't about to beg his ass. I hoped that wasn't what he was thinking.

"Shut the fuck up," he said loudly. Prison guards could be assholes for real. That guard felt the need to be a dick head to me just because he could. It didn't make no sense. "Move away from the bars."

I took a step back from the bars and he radioed for my cell to be open. We did the usual procedure while my hands were handcuffed behind my back. We headed to the part of the jail where the medical area was.

"You fuckin' junkies," said the guard in disgust. He was escorting me after getting someone to cover him.

"I ain't no junkie," I snapped back at his ass.

"Yeah whatever," he said. "I done seen enough of y'all to know the signs. You look like a fucking zombie. If you had a mirror and could see what I see you'd know you looked like one of them shits from The Walking Dead or something. I almost left you in your cell but if you'd have died it would have been a lot of paperwork for me to fill out."

I didn't respond to that. I wanted to say something to his ass and if my hands weren't handcuffed, I'd have smacked the shit out of him for talking to me like that. If we were on the streets that nigga would never be able to see me. I wasn't trying to become one of those mysterious ass prison deaths though so I kept my mouth shut as we walked.

We got to medical and he left me there in care of a doctor and the guard on duty there. This one dude was sleeping but he had stitches on his face. Someone had slashed the whole side of his face and given him a buck fifty. I needed to get my ass outta jail before the same thing happened to me. I wasn't tryin' to have to bring hell on these niggas in the jail if I got touched.

It was after lights out so they had less of a crew. There were only two doctors in there, one male and the other was female. The female doctor came over to me. She was kind of bad, one of those uppity Spanish type of chicks. She had dark brown hair, thick eyebrows that were shaped up, a thin waist and a nice set of tits too.

"So Mr. Gardner, what brings you here this evening?" she asked. "My name is Dr. Santana and it's very nice to meet you."

I immediately regretted what I had thought about her. In jail the people that worked there usually didn't treat you like you were a real person. Every now and then you could find a bleeding heart who would come in trying to save niggas. I'd seen a couple of them over the years and stuff. This doctor didn't seem like that type though.

"Nice to meet you," I said to her. I flashed her a smile. On the streets I probably could have bagged her ass if I wanted but inside of there I was just another inmate to her. "My heart's been beating mad fast and shit like that. My stomach is all fucked up. I feel like I'm getting the flu."

"The flu, huh?" she asked. She looked like she wanted to roll her eyes but she was professional. She had a little spark in her eyes.

Dr. Santana went ahead and did the whole check of my vitals. She was cool about it, even talking to me a little bit while she did it. It was cool for an authority figure to treat me like a normal person instead of just some prisoner. I knew that guards and people that worked here had to learn not to share personal information so she had only told me simple stuff and nothing really personal.

"So what's going on?" I asked her. I'd been in there for a little over an hour. I wasn't in a rush though. It wasn't like I had anywhere to go or be.

"Well Mr. Gardner, your vital levels were a little higher than I expected. Your heart rate is elevated. Your blood pressure is very high," she said. "I'm going to give you some medicine help you out with that but you're not at the point where much will help you."

"What does that mean?" I asked. She made it sound like I was dying or something.

She looked at me confused. "You're going through withdrawal. I'm sure that's not a surprise for you," she said.

"Kind of," I said. "I ain't never had this happen to me before."

"Oh really?" she asked it like she didn't believe me. "Well, this isn't one of those things that gets better over time. Every time you go through this it's going to be as bad as the time before it. You should really quit for good when you leave here."

"That's the plan," I said. She handed me a cup of water and another cup with a pill in it.

"Take that," she said. "The pill will lower your blood pressure. I want to keep you here overnight just to make sure it drops. If it spikes during your sleep that could be dangerous."

"I'm cool with that," I said. "The beds in here gotta be more comfortable than the one I sleep on."

"For sure," she said with a slight smile

That night I laid in the hospital wing. I'd convinced Dr. Santana to give me some painkillers too. The combination of the drugs was enough to help me get to sleep that night. I drifted off to sleep and dreamed of the day that I was back on top.

CHAPTER 3

Jericka

I t was the morning after work. After Marco and I left one another I headed back out. I did a couple more dances and made some more money. When I left I had a decent amount of money and felt good about it. I hoped that Hov's bail wasn't anything too crazy though. I though. I figured I'd have enough to pay it though. I also had a couple of other bills that I needed to pay. Working in a business where I got cash every night instead of a paycheck was certainly something good for my bills. I never wanted to be in a position where I didn't have enough. I sacrificed as best as I could.

I was glad that my mother didn't have to work that day. I was able to sleep in for a change and I planned on taking full advantage of it. I slept till almost 11 in the morning. When I did finally wake up I just laid in bed for a little while, enjoying the peace in the house. I'd make myself some breakfast and then go get Jasheem. Maybe I'd take him to the park or something instead of sitting in the house like always.

I was in the kitchen making my breakfast of bacon, eggs, and whole wheat toast, when my phone rang. I thought it was Hov calling again but it turned out to be Tamika, my best friend. I answered the call and plugged in my headphones.

"Good morning," I answered the phone.

"Morning," she said. "How are you?"

"Girl I'm good," I answered. "What about you?"

"Can't complain," she said. "Where you at? It sounds like you still in the house."

"Yeah, I don't have to pick Jasheem up until later cause my mother doesn't have work this morning," I explained.

"Well that's good at least," Tamika said.

"Yeah, I'm in here now making myself some breakfast," I said.

"That's good. You heard from Hov? You got the money for his bail yet?" she asked me. "Breakfast sounds good. I might stop by."

"You know you're always welcome here." I started whipping up some eggs in a bowl. "I think I got the bail money," I told her. "I can't say for sure though cause we don't know how much it's gonna be. I'm hoping it ain't too much cause then I might have to ask my mother and I'm not tryin to do that."

"True," she agreed with me. "I got a question for you."

"What is it?" I asked.

"Did you run into that dude Marco again?"

"Yeah, why?" I asked. "And before you even try and joke like you did before, nothing happened. I danced for him, he tipped, we talked, that was it. I couldn't even really bring myself to speak to him when I called him the other day."

"Nah, it's cool," she said. "I was asking cause I did a little digging into him."

"Oh really?" She definitely had my full attention now. I had been wondering about

Marco. It was like he just came from nowhere. "What'd you hear?"

"It was a whole lot of shit," she said. "I was doing Tanisha's hair and she put me on to it all."

"Well don't keep my ass waiting. I wanna hear all about it," I told her. I was definitely more than eager to hear all about Marco. It was like he'd just popped into my little world from out of the blue.

"Ok, so you remember a couple of months ago when Daquan got locked up, right?" She asked. I remembered when that happened. My ears were always to the streets. I wasn't out there like I was when Hov was in charge but I still kept up with a lot of the shit that went on.

After Hov became addicted, it was like some shit out of a movie. He'd been running everything with an iron fist so when he fell off, it created a vacuum. A lot of people felt like it was their time to step up and run the game. The one who was the most successful was Daquan and his crew. They took over most of Hov's old territory. The only problem was that they weren't strong enough to do it all the way that Hov had done. Daquan got locked up almost a year ago.

The streets had been quiet for the most part until a few weeks ago.

"Yeah, I remember," I said. "What does that have to do with Marco?"

"Hold on. I'm getting there," she said. I swear that Taimka could have had a TV or radio show or something. My girl knew how to tell a story like nobody I knew. "Anyways, so Tanisha tells me that Marco is Daquan's brother."

"What?" I was surprised as hell. I knew that Marco had just gotten out of jail and had a brother but I didn't think it was Daquan. The world was a small ass place.

"Yup," she said. "I was surprised too. So anyways, she tells me that Marco and Daquan are brothers. Marco is a little older than Daquan."

Daquan's crew was known to be vicious but fair. They didn't fuck with people unless it was necessary but every now and then they made some noise on the streets. It was a lot when Daquan got locked up cause nobody thought he would fall so quickly.

"Ok, so we know about his family. What else you find out about him?" I asked her.

"Marco is the real deal," said Tamika. "Word is he came out and came to Chicago to take over what Daquan had and he's taking it. He got all of Daquan's territory and he's taking other people's too. You heard about Rodney's little spot getting shot up right? That was Marco's people taking over. He's the real thing."

"Wow," was all I could say. Rodney was a little sneak thief that everyone in the hood knew. He was young, but cool. He had a tendency to rip people off when it came to gambling but never for any real money. Word on the street was that somebody had shot him in the foot and killed some of his people. Rodney had a couple of corners under his control. It was nothing major though. He and his crew only made enough money to keep throwing their baby mother's some money so I was surprised when I heard about him getting shot cause it seemed like a waste of time cause they were so small time.

"Yeah, I know," she said. "It's crazy cause I was just saying to someone the other day how it just felt like something was happening on the streets."

"I know. I was thinking the same thing," I said. "What made them go after Rodney?"

"From what I heard, Rodney's ass tried to get cute with Marco and he wasn't having it. Rodney works for Marco now. Apparently he wanted the territory cause he's about to go after Lil J and the rest of them cause they got the blocks on the other side of Rodney."

"The streets are about to be on fire," I said. That was always the part of this life that I hated the most: all the violence. I didn't want people to get hurt but it seemed like it was almost inevitable in the game.

"Word," she said. "It also doesn't sound like Marco just popped up. You know how Chicago is. We don't just open up to strangers and stuff so Marco's name must already be ringing bells on the street."

"True," I said. "It's so crazy cause he just seemed so regular in person."

"What you mean?" She asked me.

"Marco definitely carries himself like a boss and shit. I can't explain it," I said. "He just moves like he's so sure of himself. I've seen him talkin' to a couple of people but I didn't think that he had his hands into everything the way that he did."

"I honestly wouldn't be surprised if he knew who you were when he went into the club," Tamika said.

I sat down at the table and started eating my food. It smelled so damn good that my mouth was watering. "What you mean?" I took a bite of the eggs with the cheese on top. It came out perfect.

"I'm telling you, guys like Marco are smart. I'm sure someone told him that he had to do his research or at least speak to his brother about everything. I'm sure they probably talked about Hov cause Marco would wanna know about who used to be the man in charge so I wouldn't be surprised if your name had come up," she explained.

"I guess," I said. "I mean...it could be true but it might not be. He don't have a reason to come and look for me." I thought about it for a little bit. What if she was right? I could be a pawn in some kind of stupid ass street game or something. I didn't even want to try and think about it.

"Who knows," she said. "Either way, Marco

is the next big thing girl. It's good that you got him on you like you do."

"Thanks for the info," I said. I ignored her last comment. Marco definitely had my interest now, more than he did before. I had already sensed that he was a boss but I wasn't sure until Tamika had confirmed it for me.

"No problem. So what are you gonna do?" She asked.

"What you mean?" I was confused about what she was asking about.

"About Marco? What are you gonna do about Marco?" Tamika was saying it like it was the most normal thing in the world for us to be talking about Marco.

"What you mean what am I gonna do about him? There's nothing for me to do." I rolled my eyes even though Tamika couldn't see it. "Look, Marco seems cool and all but you know I can't just let Hov down."

"Let Hov down? What about Hov dragging you down?" Tamika said.

"It's too early for us to get into this, T," I said. Tamika made it clear on a bunch of different occasions that she didn't care for the new Hov. I couldn't blame her though. It was strange to defend him from people, because I also agreed with a lot of what they all said about him. I think on some levels, they were right.

"You right. I'll drop it," she said. "So how is Hov?"

"I don't know," I said truthfully. "I haven't really been speaking to him like that."

"He ain't call?" She asked.

"Nah, he's called. I just ain't answer," I admitted. It wasn't a pretty truth but I could be honest with Tamika.

"Why not? You keep talking about him and stuff. I'd of thought that you'd have been talking to him every time his ass called," she said.

"I know," I said. "I don't know what it is. I wanna talk to him. It's only been a few days but I miss him."

"I feel you," she said. "So why don't you guys speak?"

"Honestly Tamika, I think I like just not worry about him," I said. "People don't know what it's like dealing with Hov at times. I worry about him more than I want to admit to people. At least with him being in jail I know that I don't have to worry about him. That means that

I can just take a little breather cause that's one less thing to worry about."

"I get what you saying," she said. "I don't be giving you enough credit for how you be holding that dude down."

"Oh I don't need no credit. You know I do it out of love," I said.

"Girl I need somebody to love me like that," she threw in with a laugh. "You out here getting bail money and shit and I can't even get these niggas to pay a bill."

I busted out laughing too. She could be so damn silly at times.

Tamika and I kept on talking for a little while. Talking to her always put me at ease. It was cool to talk to someone who just got you as a person and Tamika could be that for me. She was a little pushy at times but it was nothing but love.

I got up and washed the dishes and figured that I might as well go ahead and clean up since it was just me in the house. I plugged my phone into the speaker and acted like my mother did on Sunday's, cleaning my house top to bottom. I was just about to mop the kitchen floor when the phone started ringing through the speakers.

I walked over to it and answered it, not recognizing the number.

"Hello?" I answered the phone. At least whoever it was hadn't called blocked cause they wouldn't have gotten a response from me at all.

"Hello? Jericka?" The person on the other end of the phone had a deep voice. It sounded kind of familiar.

"Who the fuck is this? Don't be playing on my phone," I snapped. I wasn't in the mood for the shit.

"Chill, it's James," said the voice.

"James who?" I was just about to hang up the phone when he spoke again.

"Hov's friend James," he said quickly. "He called me and gave me your number."

I rolled my eyes. Hov had some damn nerve having one of his little druggie buddies calling my phone. He knew how I felt about people having my damn number.

"For what?" I asked.

"He wants you to call him or go visit him," James said. "Between you and me I think he's startin' to go through detox."

"Oh ok. I'm sure he's fine," I said. "Well, thanks for calling. I'll speak to him." I hung up the phone. I was familiar with James cause he was friends with Hov but we weren't cool enough for me to get into my feelings on the phone with.

I decided right then and there that I just needed to go ahead and see Hov. It didn't make any sense for me not to talk to him. I was definitely worried with the stuff that James had just told me. As sad as it was, Hov had never really had to do a regular detox like this before. He was always away at rehab and they were able to help him through it with some medicine. I hoped that if it did get that bad that the prison would give him something to help him through it but I wasn't getting my hopes up.

I finished cleaning up and jumped in the shower. I knew how jails could be sometimes when it came to treating the visitors like they were prisoners themselves too. I put on a pair of boyfriend jeans cause I wanted something that fit a little more loosely, not that much could be done to cover my ass. I put on a simple white V-neck t-shirt and brought my sunglasses and a purse. I made to double check that I had my ID. I didn't need no bullshit when I got there.

On the way to the jail I text my mother and

asked if everything was alright. She told me that it was fine if I came to pick up Jasheem that evening because she'd taken him to a play date with somebody from the church. I was really grateful to have that old lady around.

The process to get into meet Hov was annoying but not too long thankfully. It was only county jail so they didn't have you go through all the other stuff that they did at places like state prisons. This white bitch at the club was from New York and she told us all about how hard it was to get in there to see anyone cause it was so big and the guards were so rude. I hated coming to jails. I hoped shit worked out for Hov because I didn't want to have to go and visit him at a place like that anytime soon.

I sat in the large visitors' room, waiting for Hov to be escorted in. The room was exactly like I'd imagined it would look. It was large and brightly lit with small round tables all throughout it. It was just weird to see because it felt like the room sucked up all the happiness or something. The walls were gray. The tables were white and the chairs were black. It gave me the chills when I thought about it.

After almost ten minutes Hov was escorted

in. I got a little emotional seeing him like that. Hov was a big man but something about the way that he looked made him look so damn small. He had on a dark blue set of scrubs and plain white sneakers. His facial hair was growing in and really needed to be shaved. The worst part of it was his eyes. He looked like a zombie or like he was in pain or something.

He walked up to me and we hugged for as long as we could before the asshole of a guard told us we had to break it up. I took a seat on one end of the table and he sat on the other. I put my hands on the table and he reached out and grabbed mine in his for a couple of seconds before he told us to break *that* up too. I looked at the guard and rolled my eyes. I'd been thoroughly searched before I went into the room. I didn't get why I couldn't touch him for longer.

"Are you ok?" I asked him. I was glad that the visiting room wasn't packed. There were only like 6 more people in the room and they were all spread out so we didn't have to be too quiet

"Yeah," he grunted. He coughed a little bit and then cleared his throat. "Yeah, I'm good.

I'm just getting a little cold or something. I was in the infirmary all night last night."

"What?" I asked. I immediately felt all the guilt rise up in me. I hadn't been answering his calls and Hov had been in the infirmary and shit. I was slipping. "What happened?"

"They had to give me some medicine," he said and he looked down to the floor. I knew the medicine had to be for his withdrawal symptoms and that he had to be embarrassed about it.

"How do you feel now?" I asked him. I wanted him to know that I cared about him.

"I'm good. Just chill. It's only been a few days. Don't fall apart when I need you most," he said. He sounded him like himself again. "How's my little man doing? You told him I was in here?"

I felt so damn guilty about everything. I felt fucked up about all the stuff with Marco. We hadn't done anything at all but it felt like I'd done something wrong. I definitely felt bad about ignoring him too. Sitting across from him at the table, I knew right then exactly how much Hov needed me.

I felt like crying. I was just so overcome with

emotions. My eyes filled with tears but I wiped them away before they could fall. It definitely wasn't the time for me to get all emotional. "Jah is fine. He's with my mother. He doesn't know you're in here. I didn't even tell my mother."

"Why not?" Hov asked. "

"I don't need nobody judging me, or you," I said. "I'll tell my mother soon though. She knows something's up."

Hov chuckled a little bit. "Yeah, Ms. Lydia ain't nothing to sleep on. She always know what's going on."

"Yeah," I said. "Other than that everything is fine. I just been working and missing you." I looked at him and a little smile formed.

"Oh you miss me, huh? So why you ain't been answering my calls Jericka?" Hov asked. His voice had taken on a little anger.

"Chill out," I said. "I just been trying to work as hard as I can. So I been going in early and most of the time I just take naps during the day when Jah is sleeping." It was a lie but I knew it sounded believable.

Hov smiled. "See, that's why I love your ass," he said. "You always thinking about me, tryin' to hold me down and shit." Hov leaned over and kissed me on the lips. It was quick but it felt so damn good. "I need you right now. Don't leave me when I need you most."

"I won't," I said.

"So how much money you made?" Hov started coughing again. He sat back in his chair and banged on his chest a little bit before clearing his throat.

"I gotta count," I said. "But it looks like a good amount." The last night at the club had been so good that I hadn't even had a chance to count the money and see how much it came out to be. It looked like a good amount though.

"Aight, cool," he said. "You going in tonight?"

"I would, but I'm gonna have Jah. My mother been watching him all day," I said. "Tamika said she's gonna watch him while I go meet you at court."

"Nah, you don't gotta do all that," he said. "When they tell me the amount I can just call you and tell you what it is."

"You sure?" I asked.

"Yeah, you just make sure you have that money ready. We don't know how much I'm gonna need," he said.

"You speak to your lawyer?" I asked.

"Yeah, he's some young dude but he seems like his head's on straight," he said. "He's talking like he knows his shit so we'll see how it goes."

Hov and I kept on talking for the full hour of the visit. I definitely felt a lot better about things after speaking to him. After I left all I could think was that all we could do at that point was wait for the bail hearing the next day.

CHAPTER 4

Hov

It meant a lot to me that Jericka came to see me. I was only in there for a couple of days but it felt like so much longer cause I couldn't do any of the things I really wanted to do. I missed Jasheem. I saw him every day so it was strange to not be around him. I also really missed Jericka. My baby loved me. She was really my ride or die. Having her come and visit me made me feel better about the rest of the day. The medicine that they'd given me had me feeling a lot better for the most part so I was just trying to chill and get through the day.

The next morning I was mad anxious. It had been a decent amount of days and I was finally about to go to my bail hearing. I woke up like an hour before it was time for the morning count. I was ready to get the hearing over with so that I could get back on the streets and do what I did. I wasn't even thinking about the drugs, I just wasn't trying to stay in there. I knew I had some decent charges against me but I was hoping and praying for the best. I had asked my lawyer why it had taken so many days for it to happen but he said that me having to go to the hospital had been what had pushed me back. I was especially anxious to get out because I was feeling like shit.

The guards came to get me real early that morning. I went with them through the whole annoying ass process that happened whenever you left the jail and went somewhere else. Correctional officers always got on my fuckin nerves cause they always wanted chances to flex their power. I couldn't deal with that shit. The whole process should have been simple enough —search me and take me to the bus heading to the court. They kept playing and doing all this unnecessary shit that I didn't get.

After a while we finally got to the court house. It was all the way downtown where all the other government buildings were. I looked out the windows of the bus as we pulled in. There were other court buses there too. I wondered how many people had come in for hearings and trials that day.

Once we pulled up, they took us off the bus and led us inside the building. There was a holding area before we could go inside when they called our names. It was packed as hell. I looked around, not seeing a familiar face. I didn't mind it though. I thought for sure that I'd see one of my boys or something but I didn't.

The only people who knew where I was were Jericka and James and I'd told both of them that they didn't have to come to court with me. God willing I wouldn't have to be in there for much longer after that day.

I finally saw my lawyer in person. He came up to me and I was surprised when he shook my hand. I'd had a couple of public defenders in the past and they were all trash. I understood the system and how it worked. I understood that they were underpaid and overworked, but they had to know that they were dealing with people's freedom and in this case, *mine*. I thought for sure that we'd be heading right to the courthouse but they took me to a holding area where I could talk to my lawyer first.

"Mr. Gardner, it's nice to meet you," he said as she shook my hand. "We've spoken over the phone. I'm Gary Levias, your court appointed attorney."

"Cool, cool," I said as I shook his hand. "So how's it looking?" I didn't need to be best friends with the dude. He looked kind of nervous anyway. He looked just like any of the lawyers that you might see on TV: white, dark hair, bright eyes. Nothing special.

"Well, you've got some serious charges against you but I've managed to do some work on it for you. You're actually a very lucky man," he said.

"Why's that?" I wondered out loud.

"Well, both the mother and her son are expected to be fine. If not, you would have most like been facing vehicular manslaughter and with something like that, you'd be lucky to get bail. I might be able to get it down to reckless endangerment or something less than that. We still have to worry about the drugs though. You were high already and carrying more drugs. It wasn't a crazy amount but who knows how it's gonna play out," he explained.

We talked for a couple more minutes. I liked the lawyer cause he didn't try and fill my head up with a bunch of bullshit. I didn't need lies. I needed to be sure of what I was facing.

My lawyer also turned out to have a couple more cases going on that day. He was standing in front of the judge for a long time. . They didn't call my name until right before they all went on lunch. They brought me into the court-room and I stood at the front next to my lawyer.

I made sure to pay attention to everything that they were saying. The judge was an older Asian woman. Her face didn't show any emotions at all but she didn't seem unfriendly, just bored. She only spoke to me a handful of times but whenever she did I made sure to answer her loud and clear. I wasn't trying to have her get mad at me and try some bullshit to make me stay in there longer than I needed to. When it was all said and done, my bail was set at $25,000.

It was early afternoon by the time I got back to the county jail. I wasn't pissed off about the bail, just nervous. I hoped that Jericka wasn't playing mc and that she had the money. I managed to get in contact with my man James and had him call a bail bondsman on three way. I gave them all the information that they needed and they told me that I would have to pay $750 in order for me to get out. I was lucky it wasn't more. I was happy that was all I had to pay. After I got off the phone with them I went ahead and called Jericka, silently praying that she'd answer this time around.

"Hello?" She answered the phone after a couple of rings. I smiled. It was hard not to get excited. I was hype as hell. I would be getting out of jail soon if everything went the way that it was supposed to. With all the days that she had, Jericka definitely had to have the money.

"Jericka? Yo, I'm back at the jail," I said.

"What happened at court? What they saying for bail?" she asked. She sounded anxious. I knew she had to want me out of there almost as bad as I wanted to get out.

"They set my bail," I said. "It's 25 large."

"What?" she yelled. "We don't have that kind of money."

"Relax baby, it's cool. I already did all the

research. You got a pen or something? I need you to write some stuff down. If you handle this today then I should be out in a few hours," I said.

I explained to her how much money she should have and where to take it to. Thankfully, she said that she had the money and would leave the house as soon as she could to get downtown to post my bail.

A few hours later, I felt like a new man. I was stepping out of the jail house, feeling like shit, but glad to be getting out. Jericka and Jasheem were waiting for me. They were sitting in her car. I was walking up to them when Jasheem spotted me before Jericka did. He started pointing at me and smiling. The both got out of the car and walked over to me.

I grabbed Jericka up in my arms and started kissing her all over her face. I hugged her tight as hell. I wanted her to know how much I cared about her. I bent down and grabbed Jasheem and picked him up. I held him in my arms tight and kissed him too. I loved my family and would do anything for them. I was glad that they were both there to support me when I needed them the most.

After standing outside for a while, looking like some BET movie, we finally got in the car and headed home. I was working hard to hide it from Jericka but I felt like shit. My whole body felt sore again. The air conditioner was on but I was sweating. I kept on coughing and shit. I should have stopped by medical and tried to get more of that medicine to help me with my withdrawal symptoms.

"Daddy are you sick?" Jasheem asked from his car seat in the back. I was surprised that he even looked up. He had his iPad with him and whenever he was in that, he ignored the world.

"A little bit," I said to him. I didn't look at Jericka but she was side eyeing me. I knew she had to be worried about me.

"Mommy, make daddy some soup like how Nana makes me soup when I'm sick," Jasheem said. He looked at Jericka and then his head was back in his iPad, focused as hell.

"Hov, you sure you ok?" Jericka asked me. I knew she had to be worried but I didn't want her to be.

"I'm still going through it," I said. I wiped my forehead which was full of sweat. "I think I just need some water and sleep or something."

"We're almost home," she said.

By the time I got out of the car, I didn't know if I'd be able to keep it together for much longer. My body was going through it. I was in pain like some shit I'd never felt before. I walked slowly to the apartment. I told Jericka to get Jasheem out of his car seat while I unlocked the door.

Once we got inside I felt like I couldn't take it anymore. I held the door open for Jasmine and Jasheem. I closed and locked the door behind us. I turned and looked down the long hallway and started feeling dizzy as hell. The living room was only a few feet away from the front door but it felt like forever trying to walk in there?

"You alright?" Jericka asked. She was looking at me with concern all in her face. I knew she had to be worried about me. Shit, I was worried about me too.

I just nodded my head. I walked into the living room and that was when it all hit me at once. My head had me in crazy amounts of pain. My body hurt like nothing I'd felt before that I felt all sweaty and dehydrated like I needed a whole gallon of water or something. I was going through it bad.

I walked into the living room and I just collapsed on the floor, grabbing my body from all the pain I was in.

CHAPTER 5

Jericka

I felt really good about having my man home. I was so glad when Hov called me and told me how much we actually had to pay for his bail. I had the money for him. It was funny because I'd just paid my phone bill and stuff so I only had a little over $800 dollars left so it worked out that his bail was $750.

The whole way home, I had to keep side eyeing him. I'd seen Hov the day before but it felt like a lifetime ago. He looked so different. For the first time, I think I was really seeing him like a drug addict. Even Jasheem knew something was wrong because he'd asked him what was up. Hov was in rough shape. He was sweating, couldn't sit still, and I saw the way that his chest kept moving up and down so quick.

When we got into the house and he dropped to the floor, I didn't know what to do. I grabbed Jasheem and took him into his room. He didn't see Hov on the floor cause his back was to him and I wanted to keep it that way. I came back out into the living room and rushed to the floor by Hov. I sat next to him and put his head on my lap.

Hov was laid out on the floor. He was laying on his side, clutching his stomach and crying in what I assumed had to be pain. I couldn't deal. I hated seeing him like that.

"Baby, what's wrong?" I asked him. "I'm calling an ambulance." I grabbed my phone and had already dialed 911 when he finally opened his mouth to speak.

"No," he grunted. His throat sounded dry like he'd fallen asleep with his mouth open or something.

"Hov, you're on the floor crying. You need an ambulance!" I said it loudly so he knew that I was being serious. I felt the tears well up in my own eyes but I wasn't trying to let myself get emotional. I had to stay in control of the situation so that I could make sure that he was good.

"Nah, I'm good," he said. He tried to sit up but just laid his head back down on my lap. I rested my back against the couch. I rubbed his head with my hands, trying to do what I could to make him feel better. My hands were wet with the sweat that was coming out of him.

"I need something to take the edge off," he said.

"What?" I said.

"Jericka, I need something," he said again. I knew at that point what kind of "something" he was talking about. I knew that he was going through withdrawal symptoms and shit but I wanted Hov to just get clean. I really wanted him to just go to the hospital so he could let his body finish getting rid of that bullshit he'd been putting into himself. I couldn't make him change though. It had to come from him.

"Hov, why not...why not just go to the hospital? They got medicine that can make you feel better and this way you can stay clean," I said. I tried to reason with him. I was pleading with him. Drugs had been what led to him losing everything and I didn't want him to keep going down this path and ending up dead or something. It felt like we were at a crossroads or something because he was at a point where he could make a choice about his future.

"Jericka," he moaned. He slowly moved his head up until he was looking at me, "how much money you got? Call James and tell him to bring me something." He went on like I hadn't even said anything about the hospital.

I just shook my head. I really didn't know what to do. On the one hand I just wanted to leave him there and let the drugs just work their way out of his system. I couldn't do that though. I was feeling way too much pain for Hov. I got him a glass of water and then sat back down on the floor with him. He looked like a big ass baby laying there. I hated seeing him lying there suffering on the floor. I pulled out my phone and dialed James. I asked him to come over to bring James something.

James showed up about twenty minutes later. I thanked him for coming and paid him for the drugs. I hated that I'd purchased them for him. How had this become my life? James had asked to come in but I told him that Hov just wanted to spend some time with his family for a little while. It was a lie; all his ass wanted to do was be with the real love of his life: his fucking drugs.

I felt like shit giving him the drugs. I definitely wasn't about to sit there and watch him smoke them. I hated the odor. I hated what they turned him into. I handed them to him and then went into Jasheem's room to check on him. I sat in the room with him for a few minutes, making sure he was good and didn't need anything. My baby was young but he was growing up so fast. He was in the room laid out on his bed, watching TV, half way asleep.

As I sat in the room with Jasheem I couldn't help but think about the things that the future might hold for him. I knew that the way you were raised played a major role in the person you turned out to be. You needed to grow up in the right environment or else it could affect you in a bad way.

Jasheem was young but in a couple of years he'd be old enough to really see things for what they are. Hov needed to get better because I never wanted to have to explain to him that his father was on drugs. Not only would it be embarrassing as hell but it might make him think that it was normal or something. I didn't want that for him. The more I thought about it, the more I wanted to talk to Hov about it and see where his mind was at.

I sat in there with him for a little while before I went back out into the living room. I was glad that Hov was off the floor. He was sitting on the couch with his eyes closed. He still looked out of it but he looked better. He wasn't sweating as much and some of the color had come back to his face. He'd looked pale before.

"You sleep?" I asked as I walked over to him and sat down on the couch next to him. He put his arm around my shoulder and started rubbing my back.

"Jericka, baby, I'm sorry for all of that just now," he said. "Dead ass. I hate getting sick like that in front of you. Thanks for taking Jah in the room so he didn't have to see me like that.

"No problem," I said with a sigh. I really didn't know how all of this had become my life. I definitely didn't plan on stuff for Hov and I going like this. It felt like so much of my life had become me just being there for other people and I didn't know who was there for me.

I loved Hov but I needed him to help pull the weight.

"How are you feeling now?" I asked him.

"Better," he said. "Not all the way but I'll be there soon. You cook anything?"

"No," I said. I rolled my eyes, glad that he couldn't see it. I'd been going hard at the strip club for him. I took care of our home and our son for him and all he could do was ask about whether or not I'd cooked? I couldn't believe that shit, not at all.

"Oh ok," he said.

"Hov, I wanna talk to you," I said. I sat up on the couch and scooted away from him so that I could look him in his eyes. I wanted him to know that I was being as serious as a heart attack.

"What's up?" he asked. His dark eyes were glazed over but still managed to focus on mine.

"Look, I just wanna be as honest as possible with you so that you feel where I'm coming from," I began. "I want you to go to rehab."

Hov was staring at me and just rolled his eyes. "Jericka, we done been through this before. You know rehab ain't gonna help me. I need to get clean on my own."

"Hov, when do you plan on making that happen?" I asked. "Honestly, I don't know what to do anymore."

"What you mean?" he asked. He was looking at me with confusion in his eyes.

"Hov, I love you, I have for years. But this stuff that's going on now should be a wake-up call to you. I'm not trying to lose you cause you got high and wanted to go for a ride or something. Plus Jasheem is getting older and in a couple of years, he's gonna start having questions. I don't wanna have to tell him that his mother is a stripper and his father is a…" I stopped myself right there. I was about to call Hov a crackhead but I caught myself.

"His father is a what?" Hov snapped at me.

"A drug addict," I said. "I don't want him to grow up thinking shit like this is normal."

Hov rolled his eyes again. "Get the fuck out of here with that shit Jericka," he said. "You ain't have no issues with shit when I was makin' all that money on the street for you to spend. Now all of a sudden, you got issues," he said.

"Hov, it's not the same thing," I said. "If you were still in the game then I'd be saying the same thing to you. I wouldn't wanna have to tell him that his father is a drug dealer." I paused, trying to calm myself down. I didn't need this shit to turn into a full-fledged argument. "Hov, I'm just trying to help you out. I don't wanna have to bury you. I want you to go to rehab."

Hov didn't say anything. He stood up and walked to the hallway. He turned and looked at me. "I'm not tryin' to hear this shit Jericka, dead ass," he said. He turned and walked down the hallway towards the kitchen.

I wasn't in the mood for an argument but I did decide that I wanted him to get what I was saying. All the things that I was trying to get across to Hov only came from a place of care. Over time our relationship had changed into something else and I had to take on more of a leadership role in order to keep holding us down. I just wanted him to look at me as a partner as opposed to a means to an end. I wasn't one of those pushover type of girls but I wasn't the arguing type either.

I got up and walked down the hall to the kitchen. I walked in and Hov was in the fridge going through it, probably looking for something to eat. I walked up to him.

"I was just in the room with Jah and I was

thinking about the future. I told you this before. I don't wanna have to explain to him that you do drugs. You think he ain't gonna see what's going on if you don't quit?"

"I'm gonna quit," he snapped at me as he closed the door to the fridge. "I done told you this before yo."

"Hov, I'm not trying to argue with you. I just want you to know that I care," I said.

He slammed his hand on the fridge and turned around to look at me. I didn't know why I was trying to get anything across to him. He was high as hell. It didn't make any sense to try and reason with him cause his mind wasn't in the right place to make any real decisions then.

"Jericka," he said loudly. He stopped and took a deep breath. "Baby, I get what you saying, I really do, but I ain't tryin to hear this shit right now. I just got out of jail and shit. I just wanna chill the fuck out and sit down."

"Hov, I'm trying to let you chill. I just want you to listen to me," I pleaded with him. My voice was starting to lose all that sweet shit. "You gotta go to rehab, Hov. Shit is getting bad for us, don't you see? If shit doesn't change, I might have to take Jasheem and go to my mother's house. We got all these fucking bills. I'm out there every night trying to make ends meet and the money keeps on vanishing."

It got real quiet then. I knew that he'd heard what I said but he didn't say anything. Looking back at it I should have been looking for a sign or something that there was something going wrong inside his head. He looked like he was out of his mind.

"Jericka, stop fuckin playin' with me!" Hov yelled. "You gonna take my son from me bitch? That's what the fuck you said? You gonna take my son and run to your mother's house? Like that bitch could help you or something."

Hov moved quicker than I thought he would. Our kitchen was long but he had walked across it in two big ass steps and before I knew it, he'd grabbed me around my neck with one hand.

"Stop fuckin playin' with me, Jericka," he said roughly. I was staring at him in his eyes and I didn't see any of the shit I normally saw there. He was high and angry as hell. I felt scared. It had been a while since he'd put his hands on me but it all came rushing back to me in an instant.

With his hands around my neck, he pushed

me out of the kitchen and backed me against the door of Jasheem's room. I tried to scream but he was cutting off my air. His hand was tight around my neck. I was so much smaller than him and I knew he wasn't holding me with as much strength as he could.

"You was gonna take my son from me Jericka? You was gonna leave me?" Spit flew from his mouth with every word he spoke. I couldn't believe we were back here again. "That's what the fuck you said, right?"

"Hov...Hov…" I was trying to say something but he wasn't letting me. His hand was wrapped around my neck too tight. He finally let me go and I slid down to the floor, tears now streaming down my face. My neck felt sore and I was sure that I'd have a couple of marks from where his hands had just been.

"Stop all that crying shit," he said. "You was so big and bad a few minutes ago, right? You was just talking all that shit about how you was gonna leave me, right? You not tough no more, Jericka? Huh?"

I thought for sure that he was done but he wasn't even close. He grabbed me roughly by the shirt and stood me back up like I was a ragdoll or something.

"I held you down for mad years and you just gonna try and leave me when I need you the most? You a disloyal bitch!" Hov drew his hand back and slapped the shit out of me with an open hand. My ear was ringing and I was seeing stars when he let me go and I landed on the floor.

Hov might have been bigger than me but I was smaller and quicker. When he let me go he stood there and I was able to quickly crawl around him into the kitchen. I stood up and ran over to the drawers and frantically opened it, trying to find a knife. I could feel my face swelling up. I looked down at my shirt and saw that I was bleeding from somewhere.

"Hov please!" I tried to plead with him but he wasn't hearing it. He turned around, that same fire still in his eyes as he walked towards me.

"You trying to get a knife?" Are you fucking serious Jericka?" His deep voice boomed loudly through the whole house. I knew that Jasheem would probably be out soon. I screamed loudly, hoping someone would hear me and call the cops or something.

Hov walked up to me and I fought him back as best as I could but it wasn't no use. He was bigger and stronger than me. He kept on hitting me, all on my face, and my body. I got in my hits as best as I could. I managed to scratch the shit out of his arms and the side of his face. He wasn't about to leave that shit looking like nothing happened. I was on the floor when I saw the door to Jasheem's room open up.

"Daddy! Stop!" Jasheem's cries broke my heart. The look in his eyes was something I'd never forget. It was a mixture of anger, shock, and fear.

I didn't want my baby to see us like this. I always wanted my child to grow up in a home with two parents but it wasn't looking like that was something that was possible. I was in more pain than I knew how to deal with. Hov had beat me before but this was the worst by a long shot. I felt pain coming from all over my body. I saw more blood on the floor and hoped that all of it wasn't coming from me.

"Go in your room," Hov said. He turned to Jasheem. Hov wiped his forehead with his sleeve. He'd worked up a sweat in the fight. His bald head was glistening with sweat. "Go in your room little man," he said as he tried to catch his breath. "Me and mommy just talking."

"Do what Daddy says, Jasheem," I said weakly. Jasheem looked down at me and then up at Hov. I didn't even realize that he had his iPad with him. Jasheem was smart and I knew that he wasn't about to believe Hov, not when it was clear that something else was happening in the kitchen.

"Leave Mommy alone!" Jasheem screamed. He raised his hand and threw his iPad hard at Hov. It managed to hit him in the leg. Jasheem turned and ran into his room and locked the door. Hov ran over to it trying to unlock it.

That was my chance. I pulled out my cell phone and dialed 911. It picked up the call after a couple of seconds.

"Thank you for calling, where is the emergency?" The voice on the other end of the phone was a female.

Hov must have noticed me on the phone. He turned and walked back towards me. I screamed loudly into the phone that I needed help. Hov came over to me and grabbed the phone. He snatched it from my hands and threw it onto the floor outside of the kitchen. I hoped that the operator had heard me before he took the phone. I didn't know what was gonna happen next but one thing was clear: I needed help.

CHAPTER 6

Hov

Jericka could be a real bitch when she wanted to be. She could be a real nag sometimes and I don't know if she even knew it. When I got up and left the living room and headed into the kitchen, it should have been clear that I wasn't trying to talk about anything else. It pissed me off when she followed me.

We'd had all these conversations before. I got how she felt, I really did. I was a grown ass man though and I wasn't about to let anyone boss me around, not Jericka or anyone else. I knew that she meant well and stuff but she just needed to respect that I ain't wanna hear about it right then and there. She just liked hearing herself talk sometimes.

I also didn't understand why the fuck she didn't wanna just let stuff go. I was down to have a conversation with her about rehab and shit but I wasn't about to do it right then. I hadn't even been in the house for a whole fuckin' hour and she was already on my back and shit. I just wanted to chill and eat some food, maybe take a nap or something, but nah she wanted to go ahead and bring up all this other shit.

I definitely didn't mean to hurt her as bad as I did. I was standing over her, having just taken her phone from her and threw that shit across the room. I wished I would have noticed it a couple of seconds before that so that she didn't have the chance to call 911. I couldn't believe that shit either. I'd just gotten out of jail and she was trying to send me back already. I didn't know who the fuck she was.

Truth be told, I hadn't even meant to hurt her that bad. I definitely mean to just smack her up a little bit. But every time I thought about what she said, I got even more pissed off. I built that bitch. I gave her everything she has. Yeah, shit had flipped and she was making the money but she owed that shit to me. She knew I didn't have anyone else so why would she threaten to leave? And take my son with her? Nah, she was bugging. I had to check her ass. Jasheem's little ass was lucky that he ran into his room. I didn't know where he learned to lock the door but I wasn't with that shit at all. When I came back, he was gonna learn some respect. I was his father after all.

I was gonna try and help Jericka off the floor but then it dawned on me that she'd called 911. The cops would probably be there in a minute. Chicago PD could come in and shoot and ask questions later so I definitely wasn't trying to see them at all. I especially couldn't afford to have them taking me off to jail now, not when I already had a court date coming up. I decided that I just needed to leave.

"I'm out," I announced. I turned and left the kitchen. I walked down the hall towards the front door. I stopped and grabbed Jericka's car keys and slammed the door behind me. She'd be alright. I'd make sure that she'd get her shit back. I just needed a place to chill out that wasn't my home.

I thought about heading to James' but that nigga lived with his grandmother and shit in a two bedroom. It was cool to chill over there every now and then but I needed a place that I could crash for a couple of days without it being a problem. That's when the thought came to my mind about where I could go: Kia Harrison's house.

Kia Harrison was one of those skeletons in the closet that we all had. Kia was a cool shorty. She and I had met one another a couple of years ago right around the time I first started getting high. I'd seen her in the hood a couple of times but I had never stopped to talk to her. She wasn't ugly or nothing like that, but I only really knew her by face.

One night James and I were out doing our thing and we happened to run into her. She made it clear that she thought I was handsome and that she wanted me. I turned her down a couple of times but then shit changed.

Once I started getting more and more into drugs, the more I saw of Kia. She was an addict herself. One time she got me invited me to her house, promising me drugs and shit when I got there. Well, there were drugs but it was clear that Kia had more than I bargained on getting from her. Shorty had opened the door butt ass naked. I was gonna try and leave, not wanting to disrespect Jericka, but then Kia pulled out the product. It was like a moth to a flame or some shit. I felt the aching in my jaw and my mouth started to water. I headed inside of her crib. We got high and fucked mad times.

Kia always had shit ready for me around that time too. I didn't know too much about her life but she must have been good with money cause she always had enough to get some drugs and have enough to share, at least with me. She definitely tried to go above and beyond for me. I liked it too. You know how men can be at times, we love attention, sometimes as much as females.

After that Kia and I had a little routine. I'd go to her house, we'd smoke, and we'd fuck. She was cool but she wasn't nothing but a bird to me so I wasn't taking her serious at all. Once Jericka found out I made it clear to Kia that I wasn't trying to fuck up my family and shit. She took it alright. Every few weeks or so though she would text me. We'd talk and shit and she made it clear that she wanted me still but I told her that I wasn't with it. Well, now that I had to find somewhere else to go, I was with it again.

I pulled out my phone and dialed her number. She answered after a couple of rings.

"Hello?" she answered. I heard some music playing in her background.

"Yo? Kia?"

"Yeah, what's going on Hov?" she asked me.

"I'm on my way to your crib. It's an emergency," I said.

"You not even gonna ask? You just gonna tell me you on the way?" she asked. I could picture her smirking in my minds eyes. "I told you that you'd come crawling back to me eventually. What did Jericka do now? I told you I don't really see it for her."

"Kia, shut the fuck up. I told you about that before. That's the mother of my son," I said. "I'll see you in a few. I'll explain everything when I get there."

"Alright," she said, "see you in a few baby."

I just shook my head when I got off the phone with her. Kia was captain of team too much. She never knew how to just chill out. I turned the car and headed in her direction. I couldn't believe that the day had started off with me in jail and was about to end with me at Kia's house again. It was just a strange set of circumstances that had led me there but fuck it, I'd deal. There was nothing else for me to do.

CHAPTER 7

Jericka

Things had happened so fast and now they were finally slowing down. I don't know how shit had gone so left with us. When I woke up that morning, the only things I had on my mind were making sure that Jasheem was good and wondering about Hov and how much money I'd have to pay for him to get out of jail. I couldn't believe how it was ending though.

I was on the kitchen floor, right where Hov had left me. He'd just left the house and if I heard correctly, his ass had taken my car keys too. Hov and I had gotten physical before, but never to that extent. It was so fucked up because

he was high and out of his right mind. I wasn't
making any excuses for him though. Hov had
fucked up for real this time because he took
things so much farther than they needed to be.

My mother had done an amazing job in
raising my brother Jayson and me. We weren't
the best kids but we were far from the worst. I
learned from her that it was important to hold
your family down. She worked hard and did
everything that she could to make sure that we
were good. She had a couple of boyfriends and
stuff but only a couple of them were anything
major. I learned from her that I needed to do
what it took to keep my family together. That's
all I was trying to do when it came to Hov. All
he heard was me threaten to leave him but he
hadn't paid any attention to the stuff that I'd
said leading up to it. I wasn't trying to hurt him.
I loved him more than anyone in the streets did,
that was for sure.

The sad part was that he left at the right
time because even though shit had already went
left, it was gonna get even more fucked up. I
could handle Hov on my own for the most part.
I just had to run away from him and stuff. When
Jasheem had come out of his room trying to

defend me, I went into mother mode. Hov rushing to Jasheem's bedroom door had set me all the way off. I'd picked up the phone and called 911 but my next move was going to be to grab a knife and get his ass. There was no way in hell that I was going to let him do *anything* to my son. Jasheem had come out of his room when I was getting beat up and for the first time he saw his father for exactly what he was: an abusive drug addict. That was something that I'd never be able to make him forget and in some ways, I was alright with that.

Slowly, I climbed off the floor. I grabbed on to the counter to help me up. I felt pain all over my body and hoped that I didn't have any bruises but I knew that the chances of that were low. I finally stood all the way up and fixed my clothes as best as I could. I didn't know if the police were on their way or what, but I knew that I needed to get to a hospital or something because I was in real pain.

I walked over to Jasheem's door and knocked. He didn't say anything so I knocked again.

"Jasheem…" I said. I cleared my throat so he could hear me. I was still crying a little bit so my voice might not have been too clear. "Jasheem, it's Mommy. Open the door. Daddy is gone."

I didn't hear anything and then finally the door clicked and he opened it slowly like he was afraid. When he saw that it was just me he threw the door all the way open and ran out to me. He grabbed onto my leg and cried like I'd never seen him cry before. I kneeled down and grabbed him. I hugged him tightly in my arms and rubbed his back.

"It's ok baby," I said. "He's gone. We're gonna be alright."

"Mommy," Jasheem cried my name out. I didn't know what my baby was going through. I just knew that he needed me right then and there.

We sat there on the floor outside of his bedroom for a little bit longer and then someone knocked loudly on the door. I felt my whole body tense up. Jasheem was already gripping me tight but he held me even tighter. We both looked at the door and I saw real fear in his eyes for the first time.

"Stay here baby," I said. I went into the kitchen and grabbed a knife.

"Mommy no!" Jasheem said loudly. He didn't want me to go to the door, probably scared that it was Hov coming back to do more damage. I thought the same thing which was why I grabbed the knife. I walked slowly to the door and whoever it was knocked again.

I looked through the peephole and felt an immediate sense of relief come over me. I was from the hood which meant that I'd spent most of my time avoiding them but I don't think that I had ever been so glad to see the police standing at my door.

I put the knife down on the table by the door and opened it slowly.

"Ma'am, did you call us?" One of the officers had asked the question. There were two of them, a male and a female. The female cop was a pretty black girl. Her hair was tucked under her hat and she had kind eyes. The other one looked like a Spanish dude in his early 30's.

"Yes," I said with a sniffle. "It was me. Come in."

They came inside and Jasheem came over to me. He was like my shadow. Everywhere that I went, he went. I told the officers to take a seat and they asked me what happened. I wasn't a snitch, but I wasn't about to let Hov have the chance to do that to me again. I told the cops everything that had happened that day. I told them all about him being high and stuff. I told them how he had beaten me in front of our son and I definitely made sure to mention that he had taken my car without permission.

"Ma'am," said the female cop before I interrupted her.

"Call me Jericka," I said.

"Jericka," she said, "we're really sorry that this happened to you. We're going to make sure you get the help you need. The ambulance is a minute away. Is there anyone that we can call to come over for you?"

"Yes," I said with another sniffle. "Please call my mother." I got my phone and handed it to the cop. I heard her call my mother. I could hear my mother being loud and frantic in the background. I knew that she'd be there in a few minutes.

The ambulance arrived and they started working on me. They cleaned me up and started to do some basic stuff to my cuts and bruises.

"Ma'am," said the burly voice of the male EMT, "overall, it doesn't look too bad on the surface. We can patch up your lip and give you an ice pack to minimize the swelling on your face but we're really concerned about your ribs. It looks like you took a few bad hits so we're concerned that they may be fractured."

"Ok," I said. I took a deep breath. "We can go ahead to the hospital once my mother gets here. She should be here soon."

Like clockwork, my mother came busting into the house like a bat out of hell. She took a look at the EMT's and the police and came to me. I told them all that I just needed five minutes to talk to my mother and grab my wallet and stuff from my room. They were kind about it.

My mother and I went into my bedroom and closed the door. As soon as it was closed all the way my mother grabbed me tight into a hug and I felt fresh tears streaming down my face.

I cried. "Mommy."

"What's going on Jerickazy? Talk to me baby," my mother said as she rubbed my back. "Who did this shit to you?"

"Hov," I cried. My mother took her hands off of me and looked at me square in my eyes.

"Tell me everything," she said in a

demanding voice that only a black mother could have. "I need the whole truth."

I sat down on the bed and she did too. I took a deep breath, trying to clear my head so I could get through it all in one take. She was staring in my eyes deeply and she was going mad long without blinking.

"Ma, Hov has been in jail for the last few days. A couple of days ago I gave him some money and he went and got high and bought some more shit to try and sell. Next thing I knew, the cops were calling me asking me to come to the hospital because he'd gotten into a car crash and had almost killed somebody, plus he still had drugs on him," I said.

My mother took a deep breath and opened her mouth like she had something to say but just kept it closed instead. She just nodded her head like she wanted me to keep going.

"Him being in jail was why my mind was elsewhere whenever we would talk and stuff. Plus, it's why I was taking more time at work, cause I needed to get the money for his bail. He finally got out today. He was going through withdrawal real bad and shit. He got some drugs, got high, and then he and I got into it.

He beat me up bad, real bad," I cried. I took a deep breath. It was rough already just to talk about it but if I was gonna tell the truth, I needed to tell it all. "Mommy, Jasheem came out of his room and saw what Hov was doing to me. He threw his iPad at him and ran into his room. Hov started chasing him. I don't know what he was gonna do."

I cried hard and my mother just grabbed me in her arms tightly. I let her hold me and she calmed me down. I knew that she probably had a lot of questions and a lot of things that she wanted to say but she just kept them all to herself. She was just there for me the way I needed her to be. It was really comforting.

After that we headed to the ambulance. My mother followed behind us with Jasheem in the backseat.

Things kept moving quickly from there. Once we got to the hospital I was escorted to an exam room. The police took my statement in there. They asked me all types of questions and told me they wanted me to be as specific as possible with everything that I said. I made sure that I was. I was a little embarrassed when they took pictures of my cuts and bruises. When I finally got a chance to look in the mirror, it was bad but nowhere as bad as I thought it was.

The doctors told me that my ribs were fine but that I would be a little sore around my abdomen for a few days. They gave me some painkillers and told me to take them as I felt I needed them. My face was a little fucked up which pissed me off. My lip was cut right along the side. Under my eyes right by my cheekbone was a bruise. It was pretty noticeable but if I did my makeup then I could make it look almost regular. I had a couple of scratches and stuff too but nothing major.

They gave me my prescriptions and told me that if I felt any prolonged pain after a few days that I should come back to the emergency room. The police said that they had enough information for their report and would be on the lookout for Hov. I didn't know where he could have gone. Maybe his friend James had room for him or something but I didn't know anything about where he lived so I couldn't even take an educated guess.

I was all patched up and we climbed into my mother's car. I told her that we should just go to her house. I didn't feel safe at home. I knew that after a couple of hours Hov's high would probably come back home, sober and sorry, as per usual. I got emotional all over again thinking about the shit. I don't know why I hadn't just decided to press charges after the first time. But I think it was because I thought it was just a one-time accident.

I'd heard stories from other chicks I knew about them getting abused and I never thought it would be me. I thought that you could always see an abuser coming. I always thought the nigga would have a crazy look in his eyes or something like that. I hated what drugs had done to me and Hov. It was crazy how I wondered at times was he always an abusive person or did the drugs make him that way.

The ride back to my mother's house was short and quiet. I knew she probably had stuff she wanted to say but Jasheem was wide awake in the back seat. I knew my baby had to be tired but I figured that he wanted to stay away until he saw that I was safe. I could tell by the way that he'd acted that day that Jasheem was gonna have a great relationship with me but I hoped that him seeing Hov do what he did didn't impact him and make him think it was alright.

We got to my mother's house and I took Jasheem up to his bed. I made sure that I talked to him about what had happened. I didn't get into the specifics but I made sure that he knew that his father had done a bad thing and that it wasn't alright to do that to girls or women when he got older. I wasn't trying to disrespect Hov at all but Jasheem was young and he had to know right from wrong. If nobody else was gonna teach him, I was.

I headed back downstairs and into the kitchen where my mother was sitting at the table with a bottle and full glass of wine in front of her. I sat down across from her, pouring myself out a glass too. I needed a drink after all the shit I'd been through that day.

"Ma, I'm going to work tonight," I said. I had thought about it in the car and decided that it was what I wanted to do.

"Why Jericka? You just got out the damn hospital," she said. "Just stay here and chill out."

"Ma, I'd love to do that but I can't," I said. "I'm serious. I know I don't look like I normally do. I gotta do what's best for Jah and I need to go to work so I can make money to get out of that house and away from him. Thankfully only my name is on the lease so I can break it and just move on whenever. We just need to get away from Hov."

My mother just looked at me and took a deep breath and a long sip of her wine. She only smoked when she was stressed but she pulled out a cigarette and lit one. She pressed it to her lips, inhaling it like it was her salvation. "Jericka, I just want you to be safe," she said after the long pause.

"I will be ma," I said. "I'm gonna take a little nap and then head out. Can I borrow your car tonight?"

"Yeah, the keys are in my bag," she pointed to the counter where her purse was.

I headed upstairs to my old bedroom. She'd updated it but it still felt like home to me. My brother Jayson had a room of his own and so did my mother. It was nice that the house was so big that we didn't get on one another's nerves with space when we all lived together. My mother always kept the same room ready for me in case I was tired and needed a place to crash. Whenever I came home it was nice to sleep in a familiar place.

I laid back on the bed, trying to sleep for the

next three hours before I got up at 9 to get ready for work. I had some clothes and stuff at work which worked out because I wasn't trying to go back to my house to get anything at all.

I laid in bed, trying to get my mind to be quiet but that shit wasn't working at all. Every time I closed my eyes I got flashbacks of what he did to me. He had hurt me before but never in that kind of way. I didn't know what to do about it. I laid there for as long as I could before I drifted off to sleep, tired in more ways than one.

CHAPTER 8

Hov

I was still in Jericka's car and pulled up outside of Kia's apartment about ten minutes later. Kia had a spot in front of her house. I pulled into it, happy that cops didn't go through her block like that. I got out of the car and headed to her door. Kia lived in a little housing complex that was nothing fancy. Typical hood shit. It was still a little on the nicer side though which I liked. Plus, even though she smoked a lot, she made sure to keep her house clean and shit. I didn't try and get into her personal life like that so I didn't ask what she did for a living or anything like that. I just knew that she ain't have no kids and was willing to cut off other dudes for me so it made everything extra sweet for me.

I walked up to her door and knocked. She opened it and let me inside. Kia was pretty in a really regular kind of way. I think that was the easiest way to explain her. She was short, even shorter than Jericka at 5'3". She was mad light skinned, like Gina from Martin light skinned. She had jet black hair that she kept in a short bob cut. She had these really pretty brown eyes that looked sexy when I fucked her.

"What's good baby?" She walked up to me like I was her man home from a long day of work. She hugged me tightly and even grabbed me so I could bend down and kiss her. I kissed her back absentmindedly. It had been a long ass day already so anything that I could do just to chill out was for me. It had been a long time since I'd fucked anything so I was being a fiend for any type of female attention.

"Wassup Kia?" I said. I remembered my way around. I walked into the living room and took a seat on her sectional.

"I missed you, boy," she said. She walked over to the couch and sat down next to me. I could feel her eyes staring a hole into my neck and shit.

"That's cool," I said. I wasn't about to try and make Kia feel special. She was already hooked on me and she hadn't had the dick in months. I could use someone like her.

"So what did she do now?" Kia asked. She rolled her eyes and huffed like she was pissed off or something. She made it clear to me as often as she could that she didn't like Jericka at all.

"Chill the fuck out," I said. Kia was one of them type of bitches who needed to be put in her place. She liked when I bossed her ass around and shit.

"My bad," she apologized. "But what happened? I know something had to happen to make you come all the way over here."

"Man she was on some next level shit," I said. "I just got out of jail and shit and she was on my back about some bullshit. She was talking about how much money she had to spend to get me out and how much she does around the house and shit. I got up and left the room, trying not to get into it with her but nah, she had to follow me. She got up in my face and you know how that went."

Kia sat there eating up every word of what I was saying. It was strange at times how easy it was to fill some of these girls heads up with shit. I knew that I was lying about how things went with Jericka but it wasn't none of Kia's business what the real story was anyways.

"It's alright," she said. She moved closer to me and started to kiss me on my neck. I felt my dick jump a little bit in my pants. "I got something to make you feel better."

She got up and went into her room. When she came back out I was mad hype. She had a couple of little baggies with her and some stems. I didn't care where she got the money from. All I knew was that she had enough to keep us high all night long.

Three hours later, we'd only done half of Kia's supply and we were high as shit. My head was all way in the clouds. I sat back on the couch, looking at Kia who was slumped back too. Her eyes were almost closed.

She must have felt my eyes on her. She sat up and looked at me deep into mine. Well, as deep as she could look since her eyes were out of focus.

"What you lookin' at?" she asked me. She sat up slowly and licked her lips.

She was moving in slow motion, or maybe it was just my eyes playing tricks on me. Kia got on the floor of her living room and slowly crawled over to me. She was arching her back and her fat ass was popping out looking like something crazy in the back.

She crawled over to me and scooted herself up so that she was right in my lap looking up at me.

"You missed me, Hov?" she asked me. She started massaging my dick through my jeans.

"Yeah, I missed you," I said with a deep breath. Kia slowly unzipped my jeans. She took her hand and put it inside the zipper of my pants. She just held it there, not touching my dick. I felt my shit jump again. I undid my belt buckle and the button on the jeans.

"You lying," she said. "But it's cool. I'm gonna make you mine one day. In the meantime, let me show you what you could be getting everyday if you just stopped playing around with me."

Kia reached into my boxers and pulled my dick out. It wasn't all the way hard yet but she was holding it in her hands like it was a lollipop. She was looking down at it and I would have given almost anything at that moment for her to just put it in her mouth. Sex when you were high was some next level shit. I felt like everyone needed to experience it. I never asked Jericka to get high or anything so she wouldn't be able to compare it to anything except for the weed that she smoked every now and then. Kia on the other had fucked while high before so she knew all about how good it would feel to her.

Kia finally stopped playing around and started licking my dick. After licking at my shit for a little while she went ahead and just started sucking on the tip, the most sensitive part. She was making that shit feel mad good with the way that she was moving up and down on it. I put my hand on the back her head and pushed her mouth all the way down on my dick. I needed her to just slob my shit like something crazy.

I didn't know, nor did I ever try and think about it, but Kia had some crazy ass dick sucking skills. She swallowed my whole shit like it was nothing she kept her head moving back and forth with a crazy ass rhythm. I threw my head back. I was high as a kite. My whole body felt more sensitive. I felt my skin tingling and shit. I felt the spit dropping down to my balls from her mouth. I was in heaven.

The strange thing about being high was that it was easy to just get stuck in a little loop. If I wasn't ready try and fuck, Kia and I would have probably fallen asleep with my dick in her mouth or some shit like that. It sounded crazy but it happens.

After a couple more minutes, I told Kia to stop and to stand up and get naked for me. I liked her cause she was an overachiever. She didn't just take her clothes off, she did a whole striptease for me. She must have been thinking she was Jericka or some shit but she wasn't anywhere near as good. It was fine with me though cause it just made my dick harder.

I got up and took off all my clothes too. Kia walked up to me slowly, making sure to wave her hips from side to side as she did. She looked mad sexy in the dim light of her living room. She looked at my body, admiring my tattoos and my body. She robbed me all over before she walked up to me and started to kiss on my nipples. At the same time she grabbed my dick in her hand and started to jerk it off. That shit had me feeling mad good. I reached my hands down and started to grab on her titties and play with her nipples. She started moaning.

I was finally ready to fuck her. I asked her for a condom. She went and got one and then came back in the room. I slid it on my dick and then went back over to the couch. I bent Kia over so that her ass was in my face. I thought about eating her out or something but I thought it would be disrespectful to Jericka so I didn't do it.

With the condom on my dick I moved my hips so that I was all lined up with her pussy. I knew that my sober mind was probably wondering what the hell I was doing but I was high so I didn't give two shits.

My dick was on the bigger side so I had to slide it inside of her slowly. I grabbed her by the hips and slowly pushed myself inside of her until I was all the way inside. I paused, letting my dick get used to the warmth and tightness that she was giving me.

I moved back and then forward as I started to stroke her. Her light skin jiggled with every new stroke. After a couple of minutes, we'd worked up a rhythm. She even started to throw her shit back a little bit which was only making me more horny.

I slapped her on the ass and Kia moaned loudly.

"Do that shit again Hov," she moaned out loud. I wasn't about to deny her so I did it again, even harder that time. She grunted a little bit.

I spent the next ten minutes hittin Kia's shit from the back. She was loving it. I was thankful that the walls were thick cause we were making all types of noises. She was moaning and almost yelling. I was grunting. The sounds of our bodies slapping together was loud as hell too.

"Fuck, I'm bout to nut yo!" I said loudly.

"Wait," said Kia. She pushed her back hard, pushing me out of her and a few feet away. She turned over on the couch so that she was on her back. She spread her legs wide and then grabbed at her pussy. She wanted me to hit that shit missionary and I was all down for it.

I got down on my knees and dug into her shit. That little pause had given me my second wind. I didn't give a fuck about nothing. I was high as shit and just wanted to bust my shit. I was working my hips so hard and so fast that I wondered how Kia could even take it. She just moaned though and made crazy ass faces which only turned me on.

Finally I felt myself explode. I grabbed Kia by her ankles, holding them on my shoulder. I put my hands on her thighs and pulled her body back on to me.

"Fuck!" I moaned. "Fuck!"

"Do that shit, Hov!" Kia moaned loudly.

I exploded into the condom and dropped Kia's legs down. Both of us were breathing hard as hell. I collapsed down on to her and tried to catch my breath. After a couple of minutes I moved myself and dropped down on to the floor, still butt ass naked and on my back.

CHAPTER 9

Jericka

I was glad that my mother had let me borrow her car from her. I barely had any money left. I'd made a decent amount when Hov was gone, but I had bills to pay on top of his bills. I wasn't about to let the house fall to the wayside cause he fucked up and got arrested. Shit still had to be taken care of.

I got to work a little before ten. I knew that people had to be wondering what was going on with me. Usually I was friendly and stopped to talk to people and shit but that night I came in with my sunglasses on and walked right to my vanity mirror to get dressed. Thankfully I had enough sense to do my makeup before I came in to work. When I got in the club and looked at myself in the bright lights, I saw how noticeable the bruise under my eye was. I applied some more stuff to my face. It looked alright but if I pulled my hair just the right way, I might be able to stop people from seeing it. I had a bruise on my side but I had an outfit that could cover it up nicely. I hated to do it but I put some makeup there too to cover it up.

I was working hard that night, trying my best to keep up my little front. I wanted to make it seem like it was business as usual. I hit the stage like normal and managed to get some decent tips. I was walking around the floor, looking for another dance when I felt someone grab me by my hand.

I turned around, ready to snatch whoever it was up, but I was surprised to see who it was. Marco was standing there in front of me. His beautiful dreadlocks hung loosely on his head. His eyes seemed to dance in the lights of the club. He had a scowl on his face as he looked at me.

"Come on," he said roughly. He grabbed my hand and took me to the back area where the lap dances took place. He paid for a room and took me inside of it. Once we got in, he closed the door and turned to me.

"Yo, what the fuck happened to your face?" he asked me. His deep voice was loud and I knew that he had to be pissed off. "Your so called man did this shit to you?" Marco was huffing and puffing. I knew he had to be pissed off but I didn't expect him to be. I guess he cared about me more than I thought he did. I was almost sure that he was running a game on me or something.

"Marco, calm down," I said. I wanted him to just relax. I didn't know anything about him but something about his anger seemed so all powerful or something.

"Tell me what happened to your face, Jericka," he demanded.

For the second time that evening I explained to someone what Hov had done to me earlier in the day. I had to hold up my hands a couple of times to stop him from interrupting me. It was easier for me to just get it all out at one point in time.

"Why you ain't call me?" Marco asked.

"It all happened so fast," I said. "I ain't have any time to think straight."

"Nah, fuck all that," he said. "This nigga out here putting his hands on you in front of your son. Shout out to your little man for trying to break that shit up. That shit is ridiculous for real. Don't let me run into that nigga. I can find out what he looks like."

I knew from the tone of his voice that Marco was definitely the action type. If he didn't know who Hov was then he definitely had the means to find out.

"Just chill," I said to him. I walked up to him and put my hand on his chest trying to calm him down. "The police are looking for him already. I'm sure he ain't go far."

"You better hope he did," said Marco in a deadly tone. He took a deep breath and shook his head. "So where you at now? I hope you ain't back at y'all spot."

"Nah, I'm staying at my mother's house for a while till I figure something out," I admitted. "That's the only reason I even came in tonight. I spent most of the money I had on his bail and shit so I'm broke." I hoped he didn't think I was trying to ask him for money or something. It was cool that he'd taken this interest in me and stuff but I didn't need him to do anything for me.

"I'm putting you in a hotel," Marco said.

"No," I shook my head, "I'm good."

"Nah, I'm telling you, I got you," he said. "Just chill. We can start you off with a week or something like that. I don't want you near that nigga in case he comes back."

"Marco look, I'm glad you got this whole plan and stuff like that but I don't ain't got my hands stretched out for a handout," I said. "I can take care of myself. I been doing it for a while now without even noticing it."

"Chill yo," he said. His voice relaxed and took on a softer tone. He was staring at me deep in my eyes. "I'm not tryin' to make you feel like no charity case or nothin' like that. I just wanna help you out. You don't gotta pay me back. I'm not tryin' to fuck or nothing like that."

I was looking at him and I could see in his eyes that he was serious. It was so weird how I'd only known him for such a short time and there he was trying to help me out so much. I finally decided to just give in and let him help me.

"Alright," I said softly. "I don't get off until

3:30 so if you're still around then we can get the room."

"Cool, cool," he said. "I got some stuff to handle but I'll be outside at 3:30 on the dot."

"Ok, see you then," I said.

Marco just nodded and looked at me like he wanted to say more but didn't. He left soon after and I got back to work. I made sure that I went ahead and did my thing that night. I was really trying to make sure that I was grinding in a real way so that I could get a nice start to saving money and stuff.

Just like he said, Marco was right outside when I left. He was standing outside of a black truck. I said goodbye to the security guards and walked up to him.

"You have a good night?" he asked me. I didn't know what it was but something about him was just appealing to me even more. Something about the darkness of the night and the all black outfit that he was wearing was just making him seem like something else to me.

"Yeah," I said. "I made good money. What you do tonight?"

"I just handled my business," he said. "I got

a hotel picked out already unless you had a spot in mind."

"Nah, I ain't wanna try and pick something outside your budget," I joked with him.

Marco cracked a smile. "You real funny," he said. "You going to get your son tonight?"

"No," I said. "I'll text my mother when I get there and let her know what's going on."

"Alright," he said. "Follow me."

Marco led the way in his truck and I followed behind him in my mother's car. I knew that I needed to be back to my mother's house in the morning so that I could give her the car. I could ask her to drop me and Jah off at the hotel in the morning.

We drove for about half an hour. After everything that happened I was exhausted. The little nap that I'd taken earlier hadn't done much to help me out. Just when I thought that I might be starting to fall asleep at the wheel, he pulled into a parking lot. I hadn't even been paying attention to where we were. He'd pulled up at the Ritz Carlton all the way downtown.

I figured that he had already come there earlier and got a room because we just walked in and headed up to the room. We got off on the

8th floor and headed into one of the corner rooms.

It was a lot nicer than I thought it would be. It was a huge room with a little living room kind of area as soon as you walked inside. Once you walked past that you entered into the huge bedroom. There were two queen sized beds and the terrace in the bedroom led to a beautiful view of the city. I walked around the room, taking it all in.

"So look," Marco said after a couple of minutes of me walking around, "here's your key. I gave you both of 'em cause I don't need one. I wasn't jokin' about none of the shit I said before. I'm just tryin' to help you out."

I just nodded my head. I was glad for him in that moment.

"You got my number in your phone. If you got any problems, anything at all, just call me. The room is good for a week. After that we can figure it out and see if you need to stay longer. Don't worry about money or nothing. If you want room service or anything just order it. My cards don't get declined," he explained to me.

"Marco, I really wanna thank you for this," I said. "I don't know what's makin' you do all this but it's really sweet of you." I was being honest with him. It did mean a lot to me.

"Nah, no problem," he said. "Like I said, just call me if you need something."

I walked up to Marco and made him bend down to me a little bit. I kissed him on the cheek. It was my way of saying thank you to him.

"I'm gonna go get my son in the morning, but at some point maybe we can sit down and talk or something," I said to him.

"I'm with it," he said. Marco nodded at me and turned and walked out the hotel room.

I walked into the bedroom and climbed on to the bed by the window. I laid back on the soft bed and just relaxed for a few minutes. I thought about texting my mother and letting her know that I was there but I knew that if she didn't hear from me soon that she'd start calling me out of worry. I dialed her number and she picked it up sounding sleepy as hell.

"Hel-Hello?" She grunted. "Jericka? Everything alright? Where are you?"

"I'm good ma," I said. "I'm sorry for waking you up. I got a hotel room for a week."

"Oh that's good. Which one?" she asked

"The Ritz Carlton," I said to her.

"How the hell you paying for that?" she asked me. She was starting to wake up then.

"I'm not," I said. "There's a guy at the club. He's frontin' the bill."

"I don't know how I feel about that," she said. "But as long as your safe then I'm fine. Now look, I gotta be at work by 10 tomorrow and I don't wanna be late. So be over here by 8:30 so that we can leave by 9. I can drop you back at your room."

"Ok, sounds like a plan. I love you ma. Go back to sleep," I told her.

She yawned into the phone. "Love you too. Don't be late in the morning." She hung up the phone.

It had been a whole bitch of a day. These were the types of days that led people to make stupid ass decisions.

I couldn't believe that Hov had done that to me. Every time that I passed by a mirror I had a flashback of it. I could almost feel his hands on me. I felt helpless and that's a feeling I never wanted to feel again. I felt like I was fighting for survival. Once Hov got mad and went after Jah, that was it, I was ready for blood. I called 911 but I had already planned to plead self-defense cause I planned on killing his ass. I loved Hov, but the man that I knew was slowly being replaced by a fuckin' crackhead who couldn't be trusted. Until he made the decision to get himself clean, there was nothing I could do.

I laid on top of the bed with my eyes closed, trying to make myself go to sleep, but my mind was just wandering.

CHAPTER 10

Hov

Ain't nothing like a fucking hangover and that was exactly what I had. I was laying in the bed on my back. I felt an arm stretched out across my chest. I opened my eyes up slowly, trying to block out the morning sunlight coming in through the open window.

I looked down at the light skinned arm and I bugged out for a minute. *Where the fuck is Jericka?* was the first thought that came to my mind. Then the shit started coming back to me like flashes in a movie or some shit.

I remembered everything that had happened the day before. I saw all the shit with

Jericka and all the bullshit and then it dawned on me that my ass was at Kia's house. I looked around, finally remembering what the house looked like. She was knocked out next to me, snoring quietly.

I got up and moved her arm off of me and got up, heading to the bathroom. I looked on the floor for my underwear but I didn't see them. It took me a minute to even realize that we were in the bedroom. The last thing I remembered was us in the living room.

I headed into her bathroom and took a piss. Kia didn't have any extra toothbrushes so I just threw some mouthwash in my mouth and gargled with it. I threw a little warm water on my face after I washed my hands too. I guess she'd have to go shopping or at least show me where her extra stuff was.

I headed back into the bedroom and there was a good surprise waiting for me. Kia had woken up and she was sitting up in the bed, still naked. Her titties were sitting there looking perky as hell. Her nipples were hard too.

I guessed we hadn't finished the stash from last night. She had some in her hand and was smoking it with her eyes closed. She opened her eyes slowly and looked at me with a half-smile.

I walked over to the bed, my dick semi hard and my mouth watering. I was ready to get high. I was still butt ass naked but I climbed into the bed next to her and took the pipe. I pressed it to my lips and inhaled, letting the sweet smoke hit the back of my throat as I inhaled. I was in heaven on some next level type shit for real.

About an hour or so later, Kia and I were still butt ass naked on the bed. We hadn't done shit but sit there for a while and laugh about nothing in particular. It was then that I had a thought.

"Yo," I said to her.

"Yeah?" She responded.

"Get up and get dressed, we gotta go," I said. I started to get up and move in slow motion, trying to find my boxers again.

"What? What are you talkin' about? You just high Hov. Come lay back down," she said. She patted the spot next to her that I'd just gotten up from.

"Nah, yo, get up," I said in a little more forceful voice. Kia had a hard time doing what she was told at times.

"Why?" She asked. I looked at her and she rolled her eyes.

I took a deep breath, trying not to let my anger or my high take over and make me do something stupid. "I gotta get rid of Jericka's car. It's only in her name," I said. "Somebody gonna be lookin' for it and I can't get caught with it on top of all the other bullshit."

"Alright," she said as she finally got up. She looked disappointed. Kia was one of them bitches that was always horny. She was ready to go whenever. I knew that we'd probably end up fucking once we got back to her spot.

Kia and I both got dressed and we headed outside. She drove her car and I drove Jericka's car. I tried to take as many of the back streets as possible. I wasn't trying to run into no cops at all. We drove to the other side of the town and headed to a big ass shopping plaza. I left Jericka's car there. It would probably be a little while before somebody noticed that the car was there.

I hopped into Kia's car and sat in the passenger's seat. I put my seatbelt on and she pulled off as we headed back to her house.

Jericka

Growing up, my mother used to tell Jayson and I that an idle mind was the devil's playground. Well, she was right. I couldn't get to sleep no matter how hard I tried. It had been a full hour of me just lying there. My mind started to drift to other things and somehow it landed on Marco.

I knew it sounded like some fairy tale type shit but he was really like my knight in shining armor or something. He'd come just when I needed him to come and he was helping me out in a way that I really needed.

It was weird with Marco cause I knew that he wasn't lying when he said he saw something in me that he liked. I'd seen a couple of the bitches in the club come up to him and try and interact with him. He turned them down. He only ever wanted to see me.

I decided in that moment that what I really wanted was Marco. I wanted him to come back to my hotel room. Up until that time I hadn't really been on Marco like that but the more I laid there thinking about it, the more I saw that there was a possibility of something happening between us.

He liked me. I could tell that just by the way he looked at me, but if I wasn't sure, I remembered that I'd definitely felt his dick on brick when I danced for him at the club. Marco was handsome, had a nice smile and he smelled good. Something about him just drove me crazy. Not to mention that he already saw my value. He saw the same stuff in me that Hov used to see before the drugs made his ass go crazy. The longer I laid there thinking about Marco, the more I managed to convince myself that I needed to go ahead and give him a call and see if he wanted to chill.

I dialed his number. I was a little nervous. It was late so who knew if he'd gone to bed or something. I was surprised when he picked up the phone after 3 rings sounding wide awake.

"Yo? Jericka you good?"

"Yeah, yeah, I'm sorry," I said. "I was just calling you."

"What happened?" he asked.

"Marco when you get done working, you should come back to the hotel room with me. You don't have to say anything but come if you can. I don't wanna be alone," I said. I didn't want to sound like I was asking for sex, just company. In all honesty I didn't know what his response would be. If he did come over then who knew where things might lead between us. I just wanted things to flow as naturally as possible. Nature would take its course but in the back of my mind I thought about how I'd had that little vision of him and me and I got a little turned on.

"Aight cool. I might pop out then," he said.

"Ok, cool," I said. I tried to sound uninterested as I hung up the phone but I couldn't keep it to myself. I threw on some soft music to help me clear my mind as I rolled out of the bed.

I got up and freshened up as best as I could. I wanted to make sure that I was good in case he did show up.

It was almost dawn so I thought for sure that he would have been there by now. I looked out the window at the sun as it started to come over the buildings. It had been an hour and he still hadn't showed. I was just about to take my ass to sleep when there was a knock at the door. Cautiously, I walked over to it.

"Who is it?" I asked. I knew it was probably

Marco but who knew? Maybe Hov had followed me to the hotel. It wouldn't have been the first time that he decided to do a little pop up on me. I prayed that it wasn't.

Whoever was on the other side of the door didn't say anything. I looked through the peephole and was a little surprised.

"Oh shit," I said out loud.

Find out what happens next in part three of When You Can't Let Go! Available Now!

To find out when Mia Black has new books available, **follow Mia Black on Instagram: @authormiablack**

WHEN YOU CAN'T LET GO 3

Jericka cautiously pursues a relationship with Marco, but her relationship with Hov keeps hanging over her head. Hov's not ready to let her go, but Marco can be very persuasive. He's everything Jericka never knew she wanted, but does he care enough to keep her out of harm's way?

Hov is desperate to get his girl back. He resorts to questionable behavior to try to win her back. His efforts, though, could jeopardize her new relationship.

Find out what happens in part three of When You Can't Let Go!

Follow Mia Black on Instagram for more updates: @authormiablack

CPSIA information can be obtained
at www.ICGtesting.com
Printed in the USA
LVHW021236180820
663386LV00003B/258

9 781073 526598